Lavender Shoes

CW00553039

Lavender Shoes
EIGHT TALES OF ENCHANTMENT

* * *

ALISON UTTLEY

Illustrated by Janina Ede

ff

faber and faber
LONDON · BOSTON

First published in 1970
by Faber and Faber Limited
3 Queen Square London WCIN 3AU
This new paperback edition first published in 1989

Phototypeset by Input Typesetting Ltd, London
Printed in Great Britain by
Richard Clay Ltd, Bungay, Suffolk

CIP data for this title is available from
the British Library

ISBN 0-571-15344-5

Contents

* * *

The Fox and the Little White Hen

* * *

Once upon a time a little white hen ran away from the farmyard where she was born and set off for new adventure. She was tired of being cooped up in a narrow house all day with hens talking and clucking, and no green fields in which to walk. There was a wide world near her, and so she packed her nightdress and brush and comb, and escaped one fine day.

She walked and flew across the fields until she came to a warm yellow haystack built in a corner near a wall. 'I could make a house here,' said she to herself, and at once she dragged out some of the hay and built a small house. It had a roof of heavy grasses and a floor of beaten soil, and a window hole through which she could peep. There was a tiny trickle of water from a spring at the door and a round bowl of stone to drink from. Seeds were in the grasses of the haystack, and all was trim and neat.

She ate her supper and she got ready for bed. Then there was a tap at the door and a brown rabbit stood there.

'Is anyone here?' asked the rabbit.

'Oh, come in!' cried Mrs White Hen.

'I'm looking for lodgings,' said the rabbit. 'Have you any room to spare?'

'Oh yes,' said the hen. 'I shall be glad to have company, I have a spare room,' and she showed the rabbit a doorway into the haystack where another room was scooped out.

There was another tap, and a field mouse looked in. 'Can you do with a helper?' she asked. 'I've helped many animals, and now I am free. I only want a few grains a day.' So the mouse came to live with the white hen and the brown rabbit.

The white hen was a good housekeeper. She swept the floor and brushed up the grains of wheat that the mouse brought in. She put them in a bowl ready to make bread. She made the little beds of scented hay and got fresh hay every week from the stack, just as human people put clean sheets on their beds. She washed the dishes and dried them with leaves. She polished the bits of furniture, a table and three stools, with beeswax which the bees gave her from their store. She made jam with wild raspberries and bilberries, and she mixed spring water with wild strawberries to make strawberry wine to drink.

'Dear Henny Penny,' said the brown rabbit. 'We do love you. You make such a cosy home for us.'

'Oh, indeed,' said the hen, ruffling her wings and making her eyes sparkle. 'Oh, I must say you do not help very much. You come in with dirty feet out of the mud, and forget to find the wheat ears. You don't help me enough.'

The rabbit bowed his head. It was true. He liked to leap and run and play games, he liked to peep at the sky, and to nibble parsley in a garden, or steal a green lettuce from the farmer, or dodge away from the farmer's dog.

He had no cares in the world, and he ran out of the little hay house and left the good white hen to carry on with the help of the tiny mouse.

The mouse scuttered in and out, carrying grains of corn, finding juicy morsels to eat, filling the kettle with water from the spring, helping to hang out the clothes on washday, but she was so little she could not do very much.

One fine day, the big red fox who lived in the rocky wood came down the hill to the cornfield. He was hungry after the long winter, and he began to hunt for food.

Then he saw something white, and it was the little white hen coming from her house of hay.

'I've never seen any hens there before,' said the fox to himself. 'I could do with a nice little hen, and white hens are the tastiest. I'm in luck today.'

He crept slowly down, hiding in the cover of long grass, till he came near the hen's house. Then he lay flat and waited. He could hear the hen singing in the house, and this is what she sang:

Oh, little white hen,
Lend me a pen,
And I will write a story.
The rabbit and mouse
They leave the house,
And you work there in your glory.

A weed tickled the fox's nose and he sneezed. The hen stopped her song and listened. 'A-tishoo,' sneezed the fox again.

'Oh, dear,' said the little white hen. 'Somebody's got a cold. Where's the blackcurrant tea? Poor thing.'

She poured out a cup of hot blackcurrant tea and took it to the door. There lay the fox, and she trembled so much she spilled the tea.

'Oh! Oh!' she cried, turning back, but the fox put out a paw and waved it gently in the air.

'Oh, I'm dying. I'm dying,' he murmured feebly, and he shut his eyes and moaned.

'Poor thing,' said the hen, and she poured the rest of the blackcurrant tea into his open mouth. The fox licked his lips, it was delicious, and he changed his mind in that moment. He decided he would not eat the little white hen. He had a better plan.

'Little White Hen,' he cried in a faint voice. 'You have saved my life. Will you honour me by coming to my home, and being my housekeeper? Beautiful White Hen, please come and help a timid fox.'

The white hen fluttered her wings and stilled her panting heart, and the fox smiled a crooked smile and lured her on. He had a magical way with him.

'Beautiful Hen,' said he, 'come back with me and help an old bachelor fox to manage his untidy house. I can see at a glance you are a good housekeeper.'

The hen smiled at this. 'Sir, I accept your offer,' said she, making a curtsey, and the fox bowed his head.

'Wait a few minutes while I fill my bag and get ready,' said she.

She went back to the house, filled her little bag with a nightdress and brush, and a spare scarf for her neck. Then out she tripped.

The fox was waiting. 'She's very skinny,' said he to himself. 'I can wait a few weeks.'

'You have been working too hard, little hen,' said he to her. 'You need a holiday and I will take care of you.'

'Thank you, sir,' said the hen. 'Yes, the brown rabbit does not help me very much. He is too young and foolish.'

'The brown rabbit?' echoed the fox. 'I have not met him yet.'

'No, sir. He is out playing in the fields,' said the innocent hen.

She followed the fox across the fields, up the pasture into the woods. They came to a big black stone. 'My front door,' said the fox. He lifted a curtain of brambles and the hen hesitated. 'After you, dear White Hen,' said he politely, and he followed the hen into the house.

It was rather dark, but the fox drew back the window curtain and there was a view down the valley. Far away the hen could see the top of the haystack, but her little home was hidden in the hollow.

'Shall I make a cup of tea?' she asked, and the fox said he would be delighted. There was a little fire smouldering in the grate and he blew it into flames with a blow-bellows.

'That's a fine windy thing, sir,' said she admiringly. 'I've never seen one before.'

'It's to save your breath, Mrs Hen,' said the fox.

He filled the kettle for her and she made the tea, using a pinch of herbs from a canister on a shelf.

'Dear me,' said she, 'your house is rather dusty,' and she picked up a duster and wiped the table and a chair. Big cobwebs hung from the ceiling, but the fox said he liked a cobweb, and a spider was company for a lonely fox.

'Baked spider makes a nice supper,' said the hen.

'Yes,' replied the fox dreamily. 'But I will go to market, and you shall have better food than baked spider, Mrs Hen. You are rather thin, my dear. You need some good food.'

The hen smiled and at once went about her work. There was a lot to do, but she soon had a clean house for the fox.

So the days passed, and the little white hen looked after the fox, and gave him many a comfort. But he had to wipe his feet and to eat his meals in a secret rocky dell lest he alarmed his little housekeeper.

One day the white hen noticed a pheasant's feather on the hearth, and a guinea fowl's tail in the garden. She was worried over this for she thought the fox was a good vegetarian.

He stayed out late at night, and he locked the door so that she could never go into a field alone.

'It isn't safe, little Hen,' he told her. 'A wolf hunts at night. He would eat you.'

'A wolf!' she cried, her eyes wide with fright. 'No, I won't go out alone, sir.'

The fox often sat reading a green book which he kept on a shelf in the house. Once when he was out Mrs Hen flew up to the shelf and turned the pages. She was horrified at the tales she read.

'How to lure a pheasant off a tree' was one

story, and another was called 'How to catch a duck swimming', and 'How to catch a sleeping rabbit'.

She turned the pages, and found the way to lure a hen from its nest, by flattery and praise.

At the end of the book two pages were stuck together, and she pressed her sharp beak between them and read the tale.

'A charm against an enemy'. 'Cowslips are the flowers of magic', she read. 'Weave a garland of cowslip flowers, freshly gathered, and put it around your neck. No harm shall follow, for you shall be rendered invisible to your foe. This is a certain cure for all terrors.'

She pressed the leaves together again and flew down to the floor to ponder what she had read.

'I am in danger,' she thought. 'I am here in a fox's den, and at any time he might eat me. I must try that magical cure, if only I can get some cowslips.'

So she went carefully about her duties, and the fox continued to smile at her, but she noticed a sharp look he gave her at times.

All this time the brown rabbit and the little mouse had been trying to manage alone. They missed the little hen and her charming company. They had nobody to tell them a story or to make the beds and cook the meals.

'Where can she be?' they asked one another.

'Perhaps she flew away because I did not help her,' confessed the brown rabbit.

'I don't think she would leave us, for she loved us,' said the mouse, consoling the rabbit.

'I shall go and look for her in the hills,' said the rabbit.

'Please take care,' begged the mouse.

So in the evening as the sun was setting, the brown rabbit set off to look for the white hen. He trotted in hollows and ditches, he visited farms and cottages, and although he saw many a hen, none was as pretty and neat as his friend.

'I've heard there's a white hen imprisoned in the fox's lair, up in the rocks,' whispered a hedgehog. 'He says she's his housekeeper, he boasts about her, but I cannot believe she stays there for fun. Besides, I've never seen her going for walks.'

The rabbit nodded his head, and asked the way, and the hedgehog described the house among the rocks in the wild wood.

Soon the rabbit reached the house, and he had no doubt about it for he could hear the hen singing a song to herself. He tapped at the window and the song stopped. The hen came running to look out and when she saw the rabbit she rushed to the door and invited him in.

'Oh, my darling Rabbit,' she cried, throwing her wings around him. 'Here I am in the fox's house, and you must not stay or he might eat you. He is out now, but any minute he may return.'

'But why . . . what . . . what are you doing?' asked the rabbit.

'I'm the fox's housekeeper, but I think, I think he will eat me some day,' sighed the hen. Then she added, 'But you can save me. Yes, please pick a bunch of cowslips from Cowslip Field and bring them here tomorrow night. I can escape, I think. Oh, Rabbit, do help me!'

'Of course I will, Henny Penny. I will come when the moon peeps over the hill. If the fox is here I will put the cowslips under the window for you.'

'If he is not in the house I will put a glow-worm on the windowsill, and you can come in, but if he is indoors it will be darkness, and you must hurry off,' said the hen.

So off ran the rabbit, joyfully, and although the fox passed him on the way they did not see each other.

The next day the rabbit went to the field called 'Cowslip Field', and he picked a bunch of the sweet flowers. Then when the moon was rising behind the hill he ran to the house in the wood. On the windowsill glowed a green glow-worm, and the rabbit tapped at the door boldly.

'Oh, thank you, Rabbit,' cried the hen. 'I will make the magical wreath, and you must hurry home to tell the mouse I am coming. Goodbye, and be quick before the fox comes.'

Away ran the rabbit like a shadow in the dusk, and the white hen began at once to make the wreath. She threaded the cowslips into one

another, by piercing the stalks with her beak and slipping the next stalk through each split flower-stalk. The cowslips were large with many bells and the wreath was very beautiful. When she had used all the flowers, she slipped the wreath over her head and then went to a broken piece of glass in which the fox used to admire himself. She saw nobody, and this gave her a shock for a moment, until she realized that she was invisible to everyone, including herself. She heard a step and in came the fox.

'White Hen! White Hen!' he called, and the hen stood still, scarcely breathing.

'White Hen! Where are you hiding?' called the fox. He ran upstairs and down, into kitchen and outhouse and garden. He could not find the invisible hen, but the hen did not wait any longer. She stepped boldly out while he was in the garden, and away she went down the path through the wood, past the masses of dark rocks, past the ferns and primrose glades, away she went. Sometimes she flew a few yards, but she was afraid the cowslips might slip. So she ran.

At last she came to her old home beside the haystack, and she pushed open the door. The mouse and the rabbit sat talking, and when the door opened they stared, for nobody came in.

The hen danced round the room chuckling and crowing. Then she took the cowslip wreath from around her neck.

'I'm visible now,' said she. 'Did you ever know such magic? My dear Rabbit and little Mouse, I've come home to you.'

'I'll get the supper,' said the rabbit quickly, and he brought a fine lettuce and some corn in a dish to the table.

After supper they all tried on the wreath of cowslips. The mouse was invisible because she was completely hidden by the flowers, but the rabbit danced and leapt with the wreath bobbing on his shoulders, and they tried to catch him by following his voice.

Then the hen told her adventures, how she had been lured away by the fox, and treated kindly, but she was not sure – no, not sure of what might happen. She was so glad to come home to freedom and fun with her friends, she said.

She hung the wreath on the wall and there it may be seen to this day, for it never faded away or lost its scent.

When the white hen wishes to be invisible she wears the garland and tricks everyone, even the rabbit. When it is the rabbit's turn to wear the garland, he can hide from the white hen. As for the mouse, she is invisible without any cowslips, for she digs a hole and hides.

The fox missed the little white hen, but one day he met a beautiful vixen, and he married her and they lived in the dark house among the rocks where a family of little foxes was born. The father fox told the story of the white hen who disappeared and all the little foxes stared at him. They hoped they would find the little white hen, and that she would tell them stories.

The Little White Hen and the Three Fox-cubs

* * *

The little white hen clucked happily as she dusted her house, under the shadow of the new haystack. There was a sweet scent in the air, the smell of hay-making, of meadowsweet, creamy flowers in the ditch by the hedge, of honeysuckle waving its crowns over the bushes.

'I wish we could keep these nice smells all the year,' she thought, and she ran out of doors to look at the sun.

The brown rabbit hopped up to her, and pulled her tail feathers.

'What are you sniffing about, dear White Hen?' he asked.

'Sweet smells,' replied the hen. 'But don't pull my tail, Rabbit, or I shall pull yours.'

'You can't. It's too small,' chuckled the rabbit, and he leapt in the air and caught a butterfly and let it go.

> *I went to sea and caught a whale,*
> *I held it by its fishy tail*

sang the rabbit.

15

'Silly young rabbit,' muttered the hen, and she went to the bed of meadowsweet and collected some flower heads like white tassels.

'What are you doing, White Hen?' asked the rabbit.

'I'm going to make scent, to remind us of summer when winter comes,' she replied.

'I can remember,' laughed the rabbit, but he thought it was a good plan.

They ran through the field nipping a flower now and then, a spray of honeysuckle, which the hen flew up to gather, a few heads of clover, some purple wild thyme from the hot bank, and some wild roses which hung down close to the ground.

Soon they had enough to fill a basket, and the hen carried them back to the house with the rabbit dancing behind her. The little mouse was looking everywhere for her friends.

'Oh White Hen, I couldn't find you. Why have you picked all those flowers? Are they for supper?' she asked.

'They are to make scent,' said the hen. 'To make a nice smell in the house and all about us, when snow comes.'

The mouse looked startled. She had never heard of such a thing. Scents were in the haystack, and who could make them last?

But the white hen was determined. She asked the bees and butterflies to tell her of the sweetest flowers.

'Lavender,' said the bees.

'Lavender?' cried the hen. 'I don't know about it.'

'It grows only in gardens,' said the bees. 'But in far countries it is wild. Our fields are too cold for it, so it grows in warm gardens.'

'Then we will go to the gardens and pick it,' said the hen, nodding her head.

At dusk she flew across the fields to the garden of the farm by the common. She slipped through a gap in the hedge and walked softly down a paved path.

A puppy met her and gave a bark, but the hen was not frightened.

'Please, little dog, can you tell me where I can find a flower called lavender?' she asked.

'Lavender?' cried the astonished dog. 'Why, this hedge is made of lavender. My mistress uses it for sweet smells.'

'Please, may I have some?' asked the hen, humbly, and the dog said she might.

She nipped off many heads of the purple flowers, and the dog helped her. Soon she had a sheath of lavender, and she tucked it under her arm.

'Will you accept this gift for your mistress?' she asked the dog. She held out a white feather, smooth as silk, shining like silver.

'Thank you, little White Hen,' said the dog. 'I will give it her.'

'It is a pen,' said the white hen. 'I have put a point on it and your mistress can write with it.'

'She is only a little girl,' said the dog. 'She doesn't write very much, but she will like it.'

Then away went the hen, and the dog rushed into the farmhouse to find the little girl.

'What have you got there, Dusky?' asked the child.

'A pen,' barked the dog. 'It came from a white hen.'

'It's a feather pen,' cried the girl, 'and I do believe it came from the white hen who lives by the old stack in the field. She is my favourite hen. I'm sure it is a magical pen.'

She sat down to write with it and the pen ran its point over the paper making pictures of hens and cocks, and hens and chickens, and writing little poems all by itself for the girl when she held the handle.

'Oh, it is a magical pen,' she cried in delight.

> *Little White Hen, little White Hen,*
> *She sends you a snowy feathery pen,*
> *The pen won't write for gentlemen,*
> *Who never can find the little White Hen.*

wrote the pen in delicate flowing writing on the paper, and the little girl took the letter to her father.

'It's that white hen as lives by our haystack,' said he. 'We must not disturb her or she will fly away. She brings us luck, my little Lucy.'

But the hen took home the sheaf of lavender and the mouse stripped the fragrant heads from the long stalks, and the hen put them into a fine lawn handkerchief she once found on the common. She filled the handkerchief bag and sewed it up with little stitches, using a thorn for a needle and the fine stalks of the stitchwort flower for cotton.

Then the three friends spread out the other flowers, the honeysuckle, the wild thyme, the bedstraw, the clover and the water mint to dry on a stone slab in the hot sun. All day the flower heads dried, but at night the hen covered them up with hay to keep them from the dew.

In a few days the flowers were dry, but their smell remained. The rabbit sniffed at them, the mouse rubbed her nose among them and the white hen took up a few flowers and tossed them in the air to show how light they were. They all smelled very sweet but the lavender was the best of all, so the hen fetched more and more lavender from the garden.

She sewed small bags from some foxglove leaves, using a horsehair to sew them in tiny stitches. Then she filled the bags with the dried flower heads, and put them about the house where they shed their sweet odour.

Now, across the valley and near the top of the hill, lived Mr Fox and his three little cubs and his wife. The fox remembered the little white hen who

had once been his housekeeper, and he often talked about her to his sons.

'The white hen used to tell me stories,' said he. 'She told me about Jack the Giant-killer, and Cinderella, and Puss-in-Boots, and about the fox who wore magical shoes which ran as fast as the wind.'

'Oh, do tell us,' said the little foxes.

'Well, once on a time there was a little fox called Cinderella,' began the fox, 'and she lived in an untidy kitchen. Her two sisters would not do any work.'

The little foxes laughed and cuddled closely together.

'Like us,' they chuckled.

'Then one day they went to a dance in the barn where the King of the Foxes lived, but Cinderella was left at home.'

'Poor Cinder,' cried the little foxes. 'What next?'

'I want my dinner,' yawned the father fox. 'I could eat a little white hen. Just go off and find her, children.'

So off the little foxes went to find the white hen.

She was sitting in the sun making lavender-bags when they came galloping, rolling and skipping down the hill.

'Three little foxes,' said the white hen, calmly, but her heart fluttered and her wings trembled.

'You go home, little rabbit and mouse. I will meet the foe,' said she.

So the mouse and the rabbit scuttered into the shelter of the house, under the shade of the haystack, and the white hen waited.

'Hello,' cried the fox-cubs, stopping near her and staring at her snowy feathers. Her yellow eyes sparkled, and she nodded her head and went on sewing.

'Can you tell us about Cinderella?' asked the three foxes.

The hen chuckled, but she went on sewing.

'Come closer,' she urged. 'I won't eat you.'

They gasped, for her beak was sharp and they were rather scared. They crept nearer and the sweet smell of the lavender came to them in waves.

'Well,' said Mrs White Hen. 'Well, Cinderella had no carriage to go to the ball, but a little white hen came from the farmyard and it tapped on a stone and a carriage came out of it. Four rats came up and opened the carriage door for Cinderella, and another rat took the reins, and two little foxes pulled the carriage. Off they went to the ball.'

She stopped a minute and the little foxes nearly burst their skins with delight. 'What then?' they asked.

'Well, she wore four shoes of lavender, like these flowers, and she danced so lightly and sweetly that the Prince of the Foxes fell in love with her.'

'Oh! Oh!' cried the foxes, and each felt he was a prince.

'Well!' said the hen, eyeing them. 'The church

clock struck twelve, and everything disappeared, and the little fox scampered home in three lavender shoes, having lost one on the way. And she sat on the hearth so that nobody knew she had ever gone away.'

'What next?' asked the little foxes.

'The Prince found one of the lavender shoes in the farmyard, and he tried to find the other shoes. He hunted up and down the hills until he came to the fox's den and there, drying in the sun, were three lavender shoes. He brought the other one from his pocket and entered.

' "Does Cinderella live here?" he asked.

' "Yes," said the little fox.

' "Is this her shoe?" he asked.

' "Yes, sir," said Cinderella.

' "I want to marry her. Bring your shoes and come to the palace." '

'So the little fox picked up the four shoes, put all four on her neat small feet, and skipped off to the palace in the barn. She was married to the Prince of the Foxes and she lived happily ever after.'

'Please make us some lavender shoes, little White Hen,' implored the excited foxes, so the hen quickly wove a dozen little shoes of lavender, while the foxes waited. Then, thanking her, they galloped home and their feet were so light they nearly flew.

'Oh father! Oh father!' they cried as they rushed into the house. 'Oh, father!'

'Have you got the little white hen?' asked the fox crossly. 'You've been a long time catching her, and I'm hungry.'

'Oh, father, she made us lavender shoes, and we can be Princes,' they cried, dancing up and down the floor.

Mr Fox was annoyed with his children, but when one of them stood in the middle and sang a song, his heart softened.

'Listen, father. I know a song,' said the youngest little fox, and he sang:

Once upon a time there were three little foxes,
All of them wore fine lavender sockses,
They kept them clean in foxglove boxes,
Did these three little, good little, clever young foxes.

Mr Fox began to laugh, for he liked a song. He could never teach his sons to catch hens. Instead they danced at night in their lavender shoes, all across the hills, past the cottages and farms, even round the streets of the market town. Nobody could catch them when they wore lavender shoes, and the dogs never chased them for the smell of lavender went with them instead of the foxy smell the dogs knew.

As for the little white hen, she was never afraid of the fox-cubs, and she told them more tales when they came to visit her, tales of Sleeping Beauty, and Puss-in-Boots, and Red Riding Hood, and the three little foxes always sat quietly listening under the light of the stars, while the owls hooted and the ghosts waved their wings, listening too.

Then back home went the little foxes, saying, 'We do love the little white hen,' as they put their shoes in their boxes and went back to bed.

Country Mice meet Church Mouse

* * *

Jemima and Jeremy were two little field mice who lived in a house under the hawthorn tree on the common and they had a strange adventure one fine autumn day. It was a morning of sunshine, and golden light filled the fields of ripened corn, and scarlet poppies grew in the hedgerows.

The little mice ran along the edge of the big cornfield, through the tall stalks of the wheat, on a tiny track invisible to the eyes of people, but clear to the bright eyes of the mice. The track led to the village, but it seemed a long way to the mice. The harvest mouse peeped from the doorway of her round house high in the cornstalks, and the mice stopped for a talk.

'Please, Mrs Harvest, are we on the right path to the village?' asked Jeremy Mouse.

'Yes, my children,' said the comfortable harvest mouse. 'Go straight on, and under the gate, and turn to your right.'

'Thank you, Mrs Harvest Mouse,' replied Jeremy politely, and he took Jemima's hand and

led her through the forest of cornstalks to the gate and the village green.

Children were running about, and there was an excitement in the air. So the two mice hurried under a small gate which had a wooden roof over it, into a large garden, with upright stones. They thought it was a garden for there were many flowers lying in the grass, garlands of flowers, but it was a churchyard, with old graves and crosses.

The two ran lightly over a gravestone, where some flowers lay, but a dark head appeared near them and Mr Mole stood there, waiting.

He shook his fist at the two strangers, who leapt down and bowed to him.

'Go away,' said he sternly. 'This is not a place for field mice, not for bad little mice like you. This is the quiet garden for good mice who always behave themselves.'

'We are good mice, sir,' said Jeremy quickly. He danced back on the gravestone and wiped a dark stain from the stone with a dock-leaf. 'We are very good mice. We won't harm anything, sir,' said he to the mole.

Jemima stroked a butterfly which settled near her and the butterfly waved its wings up and down with pleasure at her soft touch. Jeremy waved his paw to a jackdaw who sat listening, and he let a ladybird settle on his fur. 'My mother says we are good,' said Jeremy. 'Do let us stay. We like this garden and no children are playing here. It is safe and quiet.'

'It is Sunday,' said the mole sternly. 'People are coming to church. Go away. You are not wanted.'

The mole dug a hole near the grave, and disappeared.

'Where has he gone?' asked Jemima.

'He's looking for bones,' jeered the jackdaw. 'Bones like yours,' he added, and he flew off with a cackle.

The church door was open and there was a trail of leaves and berries and broken stalks of flowers, with here and there a poppy and a rose head. Jeremy and Jemima Mouse entered the porch, and leapt down a step into the great empty church.

There were flowers everywhere, for it was the Harvest Festival and the decorators had finished their work. 'How pretty it is,' whispered Jemima, looking round at the chrysanthemums on the font, and the dahlias decorating a little wooden house which had a flight of wooden stairs. 'A house of flowers!'

Jeremy ran up the stairs to the pulpit and gazed over the edge at the church below. There was a big sheaf of corn on the ledge and he ate some ears of wheat and tossed a few down to Jemima below.

'What a nice little house,' said he, 'I could go to sleep here,' and he ran back to his sister. She had found a long loaf of crusty bread, freshly baked, resting against a stone figure of a sleeping man. She nibbled a little and found it very good. Then she climbed up to look at the statue. The stone man's feet rested on the back of a little dog, and the dog seemed to lick its lips when it saw Jemima perched there. 'Poor little dog,' said Jemima. She ate more of the wheat ears which hung in tassels from each wooden pew. There was a sweet smell everywhere, and plenty of food for a hundred mice.

'This is like a storehouse of food,' said Jeremy, as he nibbled some red berries and swung on the cornstalks. They bit the edges of a prayer-book and tasted the wool of an embroidered kneeler. They skated on a brass tablet let into the floor and admired their own faces reflected there.

'It could be brighter,' said Jemima. 'Let us polish it.'

She took out her tiny leafy handkerchief and rubbed the brass, and Jeremy removed his scarf and polished too. Soon the brass was bright as gold, and the words on it shone as never before. They were so busy that they did not notice someone was watching them.

'What are you doing here?' asked a cross voice, with a squeak in it. 'What do you think you are doing in our church, you bold little field mice?'

A black mouse, thin and tall, in a black coat and black leather boots came down the aisle and stood over them.

31

'Why do you come to our church, to bring your untidy ways? Why do you come here and eat our feast, that we have only once a year, when there are many poor thin church mice waiting to come and feast?'

'Please, sir, please, sir, we are very sorry, sir. We didn't know,' stammered Jemima. 'We saw the door open and here are the grains of corn from our cornfields, where we live.'

'This is our special day,' growled the church mouse. 'No food on ordinary days, no wheat-fields, or loaves of bread. We starve and we have to nibble the hymn-books and hassocks, the floor polish and the fringes on the cloths, and the crumbs the choir-boys drop for us,' said the old weary church mouse.

Jemima felt so sorry that tears came into her eyes.

'You have polished that brass plate very well,' said the church mouse, relenting as he saw her sorrow. 'If you polish the candlesticks over yonder, the Vicar will be pleased.'

'Yes, sir,' said Jeremy and Jemima, and they pattered quickly down the aisle to the chancel and ran up the big brass candlesticks to polish them.

They were busily working on these when the church bells rang out a merry peal, and the doors were opened wide. Into the church came people, all smiling with happiness to see the flowers and wheat sheaves. Jeremy and Jemima polished as quickly as they could, scurrying up and down, and nobody saw them. Now and then they took a nibble of the wax candle, but a man came across to light the candles and the two mice ran swiftly to the ground and hid in corners.

Down in the chancel they saw a tiny black flag waving on the church floor, a little black wing which fluttered piteously, and they heard a faint squeak. 'Help! Help! Help!' was the cry.

Jemima went to look and she saw a baby bat which had hurt its wing and could not fly.

Quickly she climbed into a dark corner behind the altar and gathered up a thick spider's web which hung to the wall.

'Excuse me, Mrs Spider,' said she to a large angry spider which came forward to stop her. 'Excuse me, but a spider's web is the best cure for a torn wing or a cut leg,' said she.

'It is the ancient cure,' agreed the spider, 'but nobody bothers nowadays. Who is hurt? Not a choirboy, surely? They have no wings.' She laughed hoarsely.

'No, a little bitbat,' said Jemima, and she hurried across the floor with the web. She laid it over the cut wing and bound a piece of web to keep the wing in shape. Then she lifted up the little creature and placed it on a flower petal. It fluttered its wing slowly, waveringly, it rose in the air, sailed across the church and up into the oak beams where its mother was anxiously watching.

'That was a good little mouse,' said the bat as she embraced her child.

A choirboy had seen Jemima and he threw a hymn-book at her, but she only smiled and sat down on it.

The boys began to sing. The organ poured out rich music and all the people stood and joined in. Jemima also stood and sang and her little voice squeaked an octave above the voices of the choir, so that it made a harmonious cadence.

> *All things bright and beautiful,*
> *All creatures great and small,*
> *All things wise and wonderful,*
> *The Lord God made them all.*

sang the people, and Jemima crept near Jeremy and said, 'We are creatures small, aren't we Jeremy?'

'Yes, very small, but they know about us,' whispered Jeremy.

The choirboy was watching them and the mice felt nervous. Quietly they stepped down the chancel and walked one behind the other down the aisle. People's eyes were on the flowers, on the lights and on the stained glass windows. They did not notice two little strangers who moved quietly like two small shadows, but the church mouse watched them go.

'Goodbye, my cousins,' he squeaked. 'Goodbye. You are good little creatures after all.'

The bats in the belfry flew out over the roof of

the church, singing with the people. 'All creatures great and small,' they squeaked.

Jeremy and Jemima crept through a hole in the door and went out to the graveyard and to the bright sun.

'Safe,' murmured Jeremy. 'I thought that boy would try to catch us.'

'We are creatures small,' said Jemima. 'They said so. Let's go home and tell our mother.'

So off they went, back through the cornfield, under the nest of the sleeping harvest mouse, among the butterflies and beetles, the frogs and the field mice, the hedgehogs and the spiders all the way home to their mother.

'Welcome in, my dears,' said Mrs Mouse. 'Where have you been? I've been listening to the church bells. It must be a special day for they rang so loudly.'

'We've been to Church, Mother, and it was nice,' said Jemima hugging her mother.

'And it was all full of flowers and food, so we had our dinner there,' added Jeremy.

'And we are all creatures great and small,' said Jemima.

'Are you, my dears?' asked Mrs Mouse.

'The Lord God made us all,' added Jeremy. 'They said so, all singing with choirboys.'

'It must be true,' said Mrs Mouse, and she smiled in happiness.

The Doll's House

* * *

Jemima Mouse was dancing through a field one day, climbing the stalks of wild barley to taste the fruit, nibbling a mushroom in a hollow, biting a juicy leaf, sucking a blade of sweet-tasting grass, when something red attracted her attention. It was not a bunch of roses or a red poppy, but something else.

She was startled, she 'froze', that is she became so still she was like a brown stone. Only her bright eyes moved. Then, cautiously she took a step or two closer, and she stopped. She sniffed and sniffed and a strange smell came to her. It was the smell of wood and paint, mixed with flowers.

On a bank in the grass, under the shade of a clump of foxglove leaves, stood a very small house. No house had been there before, and this was different from every house Jemima knew. It was not a mouse's house, or a toad's castle, or a mole's heap of soil hiding his fort, or a harvest mouse's round nest woven in the cornstalks. It was a real little house made of wood with four glass windows and a red roof, a chimney and a green front door. It was a house for a very small human.

'Who lives here?' wondered Jemima Mouse, but she dare not tap on the little brass knocker or open the wee door or peep in at a window.

Instead she dashed away to find her brother Jeremy Mouse. Jeremy was climbing a tree. It was only a hawthorn bush but he wanted to eat the juicy red berries which mice and children find so tempting. These 'haws' taste like bread and he called them 'Mouse-bread'.

He saw Jemima running across the grass, and he hid until she was near, when he leapt down to frighten her.

'Boo!' he shouted in a loud squeak as he dropped by her side.

'Oh Jeremy!' she panted. 'I have found a house. Come quickly and look at it.'

'A house?' echoed Jeremy. 'What kind of house? Some houses are dangerous, Jemima,' said he.

'Not this house. It is too little. It is a fairy house,' said Jemima, taking her brother's arm and holding the lively mouse.

They walked away, along the tiny field tracks made by mice and frogs and spiders, paths invisible to humans but clear to the small animals.

'It's a witch's house,' said Jeremy when he saw the little red roof and the green door and glass windows.

'Nonsense,' said Jemima. 'It's a fairy house, where pretty fairies live. Let's go in.'

They waited and watched, but nothing stirred. So they tiptoed silently to the green door and tapped. Nobody came. Nobody stirred in the little house and a butterfly perched on the red roof and fanned her wings.

'Quite safe,' she murmured softly.

They pushed the door and it swung open, and they saw a little hall and a flight of wooden stairs.

'Let's both go in together,' they whispered, and

they boldly walked in and the door shut behind them.

They ran up the narrow stairs and pushed open a door. It led to a nursery with some little toys. There was a wooden rocking-horse and a basket, and some boxes containing seeds. They tasted the seeds and liked them. They climbed on the rocking-horse and swayed to and fro. Then they looked at two little beds, side by side. Each had a white sheet and a coloured bedcover with a lace edge, and a fine downy pillow.

'Oh,' sighed Jemima, 'nobody here and all for us. Oh Jeremy! What lovely beds!'

They sprang on the beds and lay for a minute curled up in happiness.

There was a dressing-table with a small mirror and a hairbrush. Everything was very small and pretty and the two mice were delighted. They had never seen such luxury. Their own hairbrush was a teasel brush and their mirror a pool of water. Their bed was a sheep's wool bed, and their toys were sticks and acorns.

Jemima shook her head with delight and nestled among the little blankets. Jeremy followed her example.

'I'm tired, Jemima,' he murmured. Jemima kicked off her little red shoes, and Jeremy tossed his brown hat in a corner. Soon they were both fast asleep and dreaming of warm sunshine and flowers of many colours.

Now there came across the common and into the field a little girl named Cora with her mother.

'Can you remember where you left it?' asked Mrs Green, crossly. 'It was very careless of you, Cora, to go and lose your pretty doll's house, all new and fresh. A cow may have trampled on it and broken it.'

Cora gave a little sob and stared about her. 'I left it over there,' said she, pointing to the bank of flowers. 'I thought it would look nice among the violets and stitchwort.'

They walked on, and then the little girl gave a cry and ran forward.

'Oh, Mother! There it is! It's safe!' And she sprang up the bank, parted the leaves, and disclosed the little red-roofed house with the green door and nothing amiss.

'I am glad for your sake, Cora,' said her mother, and added softly, 'and for mine, too. I like this little house.'

The child picked up the house and wiped off the dew and moisture. It looked perfectly all right. No damage was done and she tucked it under her arm and went back home with her mother. They put the doll's house on the kitchen table to dry and left it there.

The two little mice slept on. The jolting had not woken them. They slept happy and safe.

A cat leapt on the table and sniffed round the doll's house, but nothing happened, and it leapt down and mewed to the little girl who stroked it and talked to it.

'It's only the doll's house, Tommy,' said Cora. 'There's nothing for you,' and she put the cat out in the garden.

Evening came and a bright light was turned on in the kitchen. There was a rattle of washing-up and cooking and affairs of kitchen work. Jeremy awoke and sat up. He whispered uneasily. The cat moved round the doll's house, mewing anxiously and Jemima shivered as she heard the sound.

'Jemima! There's a noise. Where are we?'

The little mouse also looked about her and sat up in a fright. 'There's a tiger outside,' said she to Jeremy. 'Are we in Africa, Jeremy?'

'Keep quiet, Jemima,' whispered Jeremy. 'Keep silent and we shall be safe.'

So they crouched down and waited, and sure enough the room grew dark, the people left and the cat walked away.

They pushed open their little door and ventured out. They could see in the dark, and there was nothing to alarm them. On the table were crumbs of bread and cake, morsels of cheese and scraps of pastry. They ate these greedily, for they were very hungry.

Then Jemima saw something wonderful. Down on the floor in a corner of the room was a tiny house with walls of wire shining like silver, and a piece of cheese hanging from a hook.

'Look, Jeremy,' she said, 'a mouse's house with the door open and a piece of cheese.'

They both ran down the table legs and stared at the little wire house, shining and bright in the moonlight. Even as they gazed at it a fat brown mouse came out of a hole and pushed them aside.

'Keep away. That's my house,' said the house-mouse, crossly. 'You go back to the fields where you belong.'

They stood hesitating and they watched him enter through the wide open door. He seized the cheese in his sharp teeth, tugged and, oh, horrors! Down fell the door with a crash and he was shut inside. He dashed to the door but could not push it open. He called and cried, and Jeremy and Jemima were very sorry for him.

'Let me out! Let me out!' he called. 'Dear kind field-mice, let me out!'

'How can we open the door?' asked Jeremy.

'Press the lever down and the door will lift up,' said the house-mouse.

So they tugged at the wooden lever on the roof of the little house. They swung on the wooden bar, and pressed with all their might. Slowly the door was lifted up and the house-mouse squeezed through the crack. They let go and the door fell, but the mouse was safe.

'Thank you, kind field-mice,' said the house-mouse. 'You have saved my life. Come and meet my wife and family,' he invited, but Jeremy and Jemima declined.

'We must go home,' they said. 'Our mother will be anxious. We have been away all day. Goodbye, House-Mouse.'

'Well, goodbye and thank you again, good kind mice,' said the house-mouse.

He showed them the way through a hole in the wall down a drainpipe into the garden. Then they ran away and after a long walk they reached home safely.

'Where have you been?' asked Mrs Mouse as she hugged her two children.

'We found a fairy house, Mother, and we went to sleep in lovely beds,' said Jemima.

'And when we awoke we were in Africa and a tiger was prowling around,' said Jeremy.

'And then we escaped and we were nearly caught in a silvery house,' said Jemima.

'And we saved a mouse from a trap,' added Jeremy.

'Then we came home,' said Jemima.

'What a chapter of adventures,' said Mrs Mouse. 'But where are your red shoes, Jemima, and where is your brown hat Jeremy?'

'We left them in the fairy house,' said Jemima.

The next day little Cora opened her doll's house. In the bedroom was a pair of tiny red shoes and a brown hat lay on the floor. The beds had been slept in, the blankets were muddy.

'Fairies have been in my house, Mother!' said Cora to her mother. 'They left their shoes and a hat behind.'

'Yes, indeed! They must be fairy clothes,' agreed Cora's mother, and she wondered about this all her life.

Tim Rabbit's Magic Cloak

* * *

It was autumn, the beech leaves were falling from the great trees and covering the ground with a carpet of russet brown. Tim Rabbit came hurrying out of his house with a little old kite in his paws. It was a kite his father had made from willow twigs and a torn paper bag he had found on the common. It had a real string to hold it, but the tail was ragged.

'Goodbye, Mother,' called Tim, 'I may fly to the moon. Goodbye.'

'Whatever do you mean?' asked Mrs Rabbit following him to the doorway on the common. She looked up at the sky and saw the golden brown leaves drifting down and the pale young moon dimly shining.

'I'm going to fly my kite, Mother,' said Tim again. 'Goodbye.'

Mrs Rabbit laughed and watched her son skip down the path and enter the wood. Then she went back to her house, but Tim trundled his little soft feet in the golden leaves, making a sweet sursurring sound, a rustle that fascinated him.

'All these leaves and plenty more on the trees,' he thought. 'I could make a tail for my kite and then I could make – yes, I could – a cloak for my mother.'

He sat down and tossed the leaves in the air and then he drew a heap around him. He fastened a lot of leaves to the kite's bare tail, where the paper had torn away, and soon the kite was ready.

'Now for my mother's cloak,' he muttered. He searched in the gorse bushes for a good sharp needle, and he found some wisps of sheep's wool in the hedge by the field. He 'teased' the wool between his paws to make a long thread, and he tied this to his needle of gorse. Then he began to stitch the leaves. He worked very hard, making

long strings of leaves and joining them together, and he was so intent he did not notice that somebody was watching him. Each little leaf was sewn to another leaf until he had a large web of beech leaves with here and there a nut leaf or an oak leaf with an acorn.

He began to sing in a soft little voice, and somebody listened.

Brown leaf, yellow leaf, red and gold,
Striped leaf and speckled leaf, to keep out the cold.
Good little Tim, to make a fine cloak,
Mother will smile and think it's a joke.
Then she will wear it and be a fine lady,
To walk in the fields and woodland shady.

He heard a little cough and he looked up quickly. Watching him was his cousin Sam Hare.

'Oh, Sam. I didn't see you. I thought you were the fox,' he cried.

'If I were a fox I could have eaten you,' said Sam Hare.

'But you are only a hare,' snorted Tim.

'What have you been making, Tim?' asked Sam.

'I've mended my kite and made a cloak for my mother's birthday, to keep her warm in cold weather,' said Tim proudly and he held up the cloak with its brown-gold leaves.

'Oo-oo,' said Sam. 'How clever you are Tim. I wish – I wish I were clever too.'

'Never mind Sam. I am, of course, no Ordinary Rabbit! You can fly my kite,' said Tim.

They set off together, Tim holding the cloak and Sam dragging the kite. They left the wood and climbed a little hill. Tim laid the cloak on the ground with a stone on it to say it was private property, and Sam and he ran together holding the kite by its long string.

Sometimes it flopped and danced on the ground,

and then it rose up and flew in the air, tugging at the string to get loose.

'Oh, Sam,' cried Tim. 'Suppose it lifted us both up in the air and took us to the moon.'

They ran and ran, but the kite never rose very high for the wind was half asleep. Suddenly Tim remembered his cloak. He hoped it was safe. So they turned round and ran with the kite to the little hill where they had started. There sat the fox, watching the cloak in a puzzled way.

'Hello, Tim Rabbit,' said the fox lazily stretching himself. 'Is this your heap of leaves?'

'Yes – yes,' stammered Tim, but Sam Hare hid behind a bush.

'What is it?' asked the fox.

'Only a heap of leaves, and yet it's a cloak for my mother,' said Tim.

'A cloak?' echoed the fox.

'Yes, you wear it like this,' said Tim eagerly, and he picked it up and flung it round his body, so that he was hidden in the folds of red and gold leaves.

'You are invisible,' said the fox slowly.

'Yes,' said Tim, and he started to run holding the cloak tightly round him and clasping the kite string. The wind lifted the kite and caught the leafy cloak, carrying Tim off his feet. There he was in the air, with his little feet paddling, trying to find the ground.

'Oh, I say. I'm flying,' he cried. 'Oh. Oh.'

'Dear me,' said the fox. 'How remarkable!' He leapt up but he could not reach Tim Rabbit.

Away flew Tim with the wind filling the leafy cloak and tugging at the kite.

'Poof! Poof!' shouted the wind. 'Here's a fine cloud of beech leaves,' and it tossed Tim up in the air and swept him far away.

'It's not beech leaves. It's me,' cried Tim but the wind did not hear as it strode through the sky.

Down below the fox stared, and then he went home. Little Sam Hare came from behind the bush, and he scampered away to Tim's house.

'Mammy Rabbit!' he called knocking at the door. 'Your Tim has flown away. He's gone towards the moon, Mammy Rabbit.'

Mrs Rabbit began to cry. She went out to the fields and she saw a tiny speck up in the sky. She was sure it was Tim, so she went home and sat down to cry even more.

Tim was enjoying himself as he floated along with the leafy cloak billowing around him, and the kite soaring above. He sang a little song which pleased the wind as it carried this small morsel high above the tree tops.

> *Here am I, up in the sky,*
> *Like a swallow, flying high,*
> *Swept by the wind, held by the cloak,*
> *Fluttering leaves, drifting like smoke.*

Then Tim glanced down and saw in the distance

the great blue sea and the little curling white waves. He felt very frightened and he sang again:

> *Please Mr Wind, don't let me fall,*
> *I'm only a Rabbit, young and small.*
> *Don't let me tumble down in the sea,*
> *Do take me home to my mother for tea.*

'A rabbit,' said the wind. 'Tim Rabbit.' It swung round from North-East, to South, and swept little Tim Rabbit away from the sea.

It hovered for a few minutes over Tim's home and then gently dropped Tim, down, down, down, like a bundle of leaves and fur to the ground.

'Goodbye Tim,' cried the wind and it blew the trees and sent showers of leaves to fall over him.

Tim scrambled to his feet, still holding the kite's string. He ran to the house, kicked the door open and flung himself in his mother's arms.

'Oh, oh,' cried Mrs Rabbit.'A bundle of leaves? No, it's Tim, my darling lost Tim. Where have you been, Tim? Sam Hare told me you had gone to the moon. And what's this you are wearing?'

'It's your birthday present, Mother,' laughed Tim. 'I made it for you. I made it myself out of a lot of leaves, and, Mother, if you wear it when the wind blows you can fly too.'

'Oh, thank you, Tim,' said Mrs Rabbit. 'This is a lovely cloak. Red and gold and brown, and well sewn. I am proud to wear it. It will keep me warm in the snow.'

She put the cloak round her shoulders and walked about the room with her usual dancing step.

Brown leaf, yellow leaf, red leaf and gold,
Striped leaf and speckled leaf to keep out the cold,

sang Tim dancing after her.

'Mother. You are just like a heap of leaves walking in the wind,' said Tim. 'Nobody can spy you. They will think you are only leaves, or maybe a little brown bush.'

Mrs Rabbit threw off the cloak and laughed.

'Leaves walking,' said the fox when a heap of golden leaves rolled past his den one day.

'Leaves talking,' he muttered as he heard a tiny voice sing '*Brown leaf, yellow leaf, red and gold.*'

'There's too much education these days. Leaves talking!' he added crossly. Wise Owl explained that it was a magical cloak, called by a grand name. It was a 'Camoophlaged Cloak', to make something look like something else to save them from bad things.

'Cam-oo-phlaged cloak,' sneezed the fox. 'I should like a cam-oo-phlaged coat myself, striped yellow and brown.'

'Ask Tim Rabbit to make it for you,' said the owl. 'He might, you know.'

The Adventure of Tim Rabbit and Sam Hare

* * *

One fine cold morning Sam Hare knocked on the door of Tim Rabbit's home. Mrs Rabbit opened the door cautiously.

'What is it, Sam Hare?' she asked. 'You startled me. I thought it was Mr Reynard, who came hunting here last night. He made my heart beat and I was all of a-tremble.'

'It's only me, Mrs Rabbit,' said Sam, and he gave a little leap with his long legs to show Mrs Rabbbit it was not the fox.

'Yes, I see no red coat,' said Mrs Rabbit.

'Can Tim Rabbit come out with me?' asked the hare. 'I want to take him on an adventure, up the hill to see what we can find.'

'You'll find nothing up that hill,' said Mrs Rabbit. 'Only the fox. I don't like . . .'

Then Tim dashed to the door.

'Oh, Mother, don't be frightened,' he cried. 'Mr Fox won't catch me. Sam will take care of me.'

Mrs Rabbit looked at her eager little son.

'If you promise to be careful and to hide if you see the fox even far away, you shall go,' said she.

'Oh thank you, Mother,' cried Tim and he clasped his stout little mother round the middle.

Then away they both ran swift as the wind and Mrs Rabbit sighed, wiped her eyes, and went indoors.

They ran down the lane and then they turned off at a gate and scampered across a wide field of stubble, towards a hill. Sam leapt high but little Tim got sore toes running through the prickly old corn stalks.

'Stop! Go more slowly, Sam,' he called. 'I can't keep up.'

So they settled down to a slow jogtrot, with the hare taking a leap now and then and turning a somersault to show how happy he was. He found a long stalk of corn and he put it to his mouth and blew. A sweet little sound came from it.

'Here's a corn whistle,' said he.

The sun blazed down and twinkled at them, making the stubble shine like gold.

'What is the sun?' asked Tim.

'It's a fire without any smoke,' said Sam. 'It is to warm everything without setting fire to it.'

He held out his paws and warmed them in the sunshine. An old oak tree on the hill held out its bare branches like arms to the sun and, the sun touched every twig and made it golden.

'I've seen a tree without any leaves,' cried Sam, 'and there's a sunbeam swinging in its branches.'

'What's a sunbeam?' asked Tim.

'It's one of the sun's children, come to play with us animals,' said Sam wisely. 'Look at it swinging in that bare tree, just like a bird up there.'

They came to a deserted house, and they stepped lightly up to the door, listening for any sound. Only the wind howled through a broken window and the door flapped to and fro.

Softly the two stepped into a room, where a broken bottle lay on the earth floor, and a mouse-trap lay ready for the mouse that never came. On the windowsill a butterfly sat in a cranny, fast asleep for the winter.

Tim and Sam stared at it, and touched its closed wings that were like petals, but the butterfly took no notice and slept on.

In a corner a hedgehog was curled up under a blanket of dead leaves. He opened one eye and winked and went on sleeping.

'Sleepy Joe, the hedgehog,' whispered Sam, and he tied a tiny rag to a prickle, but Tim took it off.

'Don't be silly, Sam Hare,' he muttered. 'Leave a fellow in peace. Beware of Reynard the Fox. He came here one night.'

The hedgehog rolled himself in a ball and went close to Sam Hare, turning over and over with all his spikes.

'Oh, get away, Sleepy Joe,' cried Sam. 'You are pricking me with your pins.'

'I'm a pin-cushion,' laughed the hedgehog sleepily.

'Then I'll get some needles and be a needle-case,' said Sam Hare quickly, and he tugged some thorns from the hawthorn tree and fastened them in his thick long hair.

Tim Rabbit grabbed a wisp of white sheep's wool from a bramble. He took one of Sam Hare's thorns and threaded it with a strand of the wool.

'I'll sew your clothes for you, like my mother does,' said he, waving the needle and thread.

'Go away,' cried the hedgehog. 'You are both crazy. Leave me, do.'

A gust of wind came flurrying round the corner. It swept the hare and the rabbit off their feet, but the little plump hedgehog only rolled in its ball and went on sleeping.

'I love being bowled along like that,' whispered Tim. The hare and rabbit were blown half across the hillside, and then the wind dropped them both in a leafy hollow.

'That was an adventure,' cried Sam Hare. 'I've never been in an airyplane before.'

'Nor me,' said Tim, straightening his fur. 'Is the wind an airyplane, Sam?'

'Of course it is. It can carry us right round the world, if we wants,' said Sam. 'But we don't want to go yet, do we?'

The wind was busy sweeping up the leaves. It caught them and whirled them round, and then sent a big bundle of the dried leaves towards a wall where it dropped them.

Sam and Tim ran after the wind, calling, 'Stop, Wind! Stop!' And when the brown heap fell they leapt into it and covered themselves.

They were just in time, for Sam heard a snuffle and when he peeped out with one eye he saw Reynard the Fox standing a few yards away.

Sam whispered one word only into Tim's ear: '*Fox.*'

Tim stayed as still as a stone and so did Sam Hare. The fox sniffed and walked on, and climbed the wall.

Sam Hare could not resist making a mocking little cry.

'Coo-ee, coo-ee!' he piped, very high, and the fox stopped at once and leapt back to the leaves.

'Somebody lost?' asked the fox.

The fox went to the heap of leaves and the two

animals shivered so much that the leaves began to quiver too. The wind, who had been leaning against the wall, saw its leaves moving, and it stooped down and blew upon them. The host of brown leaves joined together like a net and rose up with the rabbit and hare inside it. Over the wall they sailed, over the fox's red head, and away to a little wood near the top of the hill. There the wind dropped them at the foot of a leafless oak tree.

In the tree there was a hole and Sam and Tim crept inside.

It was a nice little round house with a tall chimney which went straight up the tree. There was a cupboard in the wall, with some bread and cheese wrapped in paper on a ledge, and a curved knife and a hone for sharpening the knife.

'Oh!' cried Sam. 'Here's a larder for somebody. It must be the shepherd's hiding place, where he goes when it rains.'

'Yes,' said Tim. 'I know that shepherd. He's a nice man. He never tries to hurt me, and he takes care of the sheep and lambs.'

They munched the bread and cheese, and drank from a spring at the door of the tree.

Sam put a paw in the water and brought out a shining bit of silver.

'Here's something pretty,' said he. 'Somebody's lost it. Let's put it on the shelf where we found the bread and cheese. The shepherd will like it.'

So they put the old silver shilling on the wooden shelf close to the knife and the hone.

They were tired, and they curled up in the cosy hole, wrapped a few leaves around their bodies and fell asleep. The stars were coming out when they awoke. The moon shone down on the cold field, and the wind blew fiercely.

'The airyplane is blowing the wrong way for us,' said Tim, holding up a wet paw to the wind's direction. 'We shall have to go home without any ride.'

They trotted away down the hill towards home, but a cold icy wind blew into their faces, and ruffled their fur to touch their skin with shivers.

Sam found a bundle of hay left by the sheep and he twisted it into a scarf for his friend's neck.

'Oh, that is warm. Thank you, Sam,' said Tim.

They drank from a tiny stream and ate a few blades of grass. They came to a cottage and on a clothes-line hung a yellow duster drying. Sam leapt up and grabbed it.

'I'll borrow this from old Mrs Moss. She won't mind, and I'll take it back tomorrow.'

So he put the duster round his throat and he became as warm as his friend Tim.

'Where did you get that scarf, young Hare?' snarled a voice and the fox sprang out of the bushes and stood in front of them. 'Hand it over or I'll take you and scarf too,' said the fox.

Sam unwound it from his neck and tossed it in the air. The fox grabbed it but the wind caught it and fluttered it back to the garden. The fox sprang over the wall after it, but that gave the two little animals time to escape. They ran with might and main to Tim's house.

'You had better stay here all night, Sam,' said Mrs Rabbit who was glad to see them safe and sound. 'Where have you been? Did you have any adventures?'

The two little animals stood on the hearthrug, their eyes shining, their breath coming quickly.

'Tell her,' said Sam. So Tim and Sam sang a little duet to Mrs Rabbit:

Tim Rabbit began:

> *We've seen a sunbeam swinging on an oak,*
> *We've seen a fire without any smoke.*

Sam Hare continued:

> *We've seen a butterfly asleep in a house,*
> *We've seen a mousetrap waiting for a mouse.*

Tim:

> *We've seen a tree with no leaves at all,*
> *We've seen a hedgehog curled up like a ball.*

Sam:

> *We've seen the wind like an airyplane,*
> *We've tricked the fox and got away again.*

Tim:

> *We flew away like birds in the air,*
> *We are adventurers, me and Sam Hare.*

And they bowed their furry heads and laughed.
So Mrs Rabbit sent them off to bed with some
bread and milk for supper.

The Ladybirds

* * *

In an old tree-stump, hidden under a roof of lichen sheltered by a strip of bark, stood a tiny house. It was so small you would never have seen it unless you raised the roof and peered underneath. The house had a mossy floor like a green carpet, and a row of little beds lined with wool, for the three daughters who slept there in their folded cloaks.

Mrs Ladybird had three charming children, and their names were Polly, Molly and Ann. Polly and Molly were beautiful ladybirds whose spotted red cloaks gleamed in the sun, but Ann, the youngest, was a dark little creature with no black spots on her cloak. She walked with a limp, she could not fly for her wings were stuck, so she stayed quietly in a corner, while her gay sisters danced and spread their little wings and flew into the meadow singing with tiny voices a ladybird song:

'Ann, Ann,' they called. 'Listen to us.'

Ladybird, ladybird, fly away home,
Your house is on fire, your children all gone,
All but one and her name is Ann,
And she hides under the frying-pan.

It was an old song, made up a hundred years ago, and little Ann hated it. She crept close to her bed and covered herself with a blanket.

'Hush, naughty girls,' said Mrs Ladybird. 'You must not tease poor Ann. She would never hide under the frying-pan.'

It was true that Ann could not fly, her wings were tightly closed and, unlike her sisters, she had always to crawl. All the same she was a happy little creature, for she saw much more than the two sisters, as she walked slowly among the flowers of the field, tasting the dew on the grass blades, stroking the flowers. Ants trotted past her carrying little sticks for the ant-hill, and they said, 'Good morning, Ann. It's a fine day, isn't it?'

Or she met a beetle scurrying along, and he flapped his black wings and zoomed in the air, and sometimes he took her for an exciting ride, perched on his back.

'Dear Mr Dumbledore,' said Ann. 'How well you fly.'

'Rheumatics bad, Miss Ann,' said the Dumble-dore, 'but you are light as a feather, my dear.'

She saw the field spiders weaving their long silken nets to catch the flies. They seldom spoke, they were too busy, but Ann admired their skill. One spider made her a fine silvery rope, and Ann played with it in the trees, swinging from it after she had knotted it to a bough. That was great fun for her.

She liked the butterflies, who often came down to perch on a flower to sip the honey. They told her tales of a lake where waterlilies grew, and frogs sat fishing, of blue kingfishers, down the river, bright as themselves, of birds and animals of river and meadow and marshland.

Molly and Polly never spoke to the butterflies, they were too proud.

'If only I had a red cloak, with spots of black, and wings, so that I could fly like my sisters,' said Ann to a yellow brimstone butterfly who fluttered his sulphur wings on a cowslip flower near the ladybirds' home.

'Some day,' sang the butterfly. 'Be patient. You will get your wish and fly over the trees to see the moon.'

Ann walked slowly back up the tree-stump to her home. She looked at a frying-pan hanging on the wall. It shone bright as the moon, for it was made of silver. An elf found a silver threepenny bit in a field one day, and he turned up the edge and beat it with his stone hammer until he shaped it into a tiny frying-pan. One day he lost it, and although he hunted up and down he could not find it. A woolly caterpillar found it and gave it to Ann's grandmother. It had hung in the little tree-house ever since and everyone admired it. Mrs Ladybird kept it brightly polished with a scrap of sand and a leafy rag for a duster.

It had never been used for cooking, but

sometimes the ladybirds put a few ears of wheat crushed with a stone in it, to bake in the hot sunshine. These made a loaf of ladybird bread.

The little frying-pan had a picture of a lady on one side, and a crown with the figure 3 on the other.

'What does it mean?' asked Ann.

'Three children. Three ladybirds,' said her mother. 'It's a lucky coin, Ann. See, there's a little hole bored in the edge, where a girl has worn it round her neck. You can make a wish with it.'

Ann waited until she was alone and then she wished.

> *Silver pan, frying-pan,*
> *Grant me a wish as fast as you can.*
> *Give me two wings and a spotted cloak,*
> *Let me fly over the tallest oak.*
> *Or give me two fins like a small fish,*
> *To swim in the pool, O grant me my wish.*

But the frying-pan only hung on the wall and said nothing.

Spring came and the field was filled with nodding cowslips and delicate yellow primroses, with violets and chimney-sweepers, little black brushes, with daisies and buttercups. Ann was happy. She could climb up the tall strong stalks of the cowslips and lie in the circle of bells. The wind blew, the cowslips rocked, but she was safe. She was lulled to sleep in the cowslip bells.

A red admiral butterfly flew down to Ann's flower to sip the honey, and he gave the ladybird a taste. A golden fly settled there and the three played a game of swinging in the wind.

The church bells began to ring, and all the bells in the field joined in the music, for spring was there.

The bumblebee brought a fiddle and played a tune, a grass-hopper came chirping to sing with them. But some people came for a picnic, and all the musicians flew away. Ann crept close to the cowslip and shut her eyes.

'Here's a ladybird without any spots,' said a voice, and she was flicked out of the flower, so she hid in the grass and wept a little. The people ate and drank, and they broke a bottle. Then away they went, leaving a mess behind them.

The cows ate the bread-and-butter, the ladybirds ate the crumbs of cake, the butterflies ate the sugar, and the ants carried away the scraps of paper for their nest. The farmer grumbled and swept up the glass, but he did not notice that a piece of bottle was left on the tree-stump.

The blazing sun beat down on the glass, and the dry grass grew hot. The tiny house was like an oven, and the ladybirds could not sleep. Molly and Polly flew away, and Mrs Ladybird took her basket and went shopping in the field. The sun shone through the glass, and the old tree-trunk caught fire. The silver pan fell but Ann seized it and dragged it after her down the tree to the grasses. She hid it under the large leaves of a dock, and then she walked away. She was hot and frightened, for her home was burning.

'Fire! Fire!' cried all the little field folk, the mice, the ants, the beetles, the butterflies, and the bees. The noise awoke the little elf, down in his underground house. 'Fire!' he thought, and he came dancing out. Mrs Ladybird was busy with her shopping in the market where she found petals of flowers, balls of dew, juicy little insects, and drops of honey. She heard a harebell ringing, and the elf came running up and down, waving the bell and shouting something that brought fear to her heart.

'Ladybird! Ladybird!' he cried. 'Where are you?'

'I'm here,' she said, and the elf stopped.

'Ladybird, Ladybird, fly away home,' he sang. 'Your house is on fire and your children all gone.'

'Oh, dear!' cried the ladybird. 'O my house! My children! My little Ann!'

'All except one and her name is Ann,' said the elf. 'And she has taken the frying-pan.'

'Oh, dear Elf, dear sir,' said Mrs Ladybird. 'Thank you! If my little Ann is safe, the others can fly. They will come to no harm.'

She picked up her basket and flew home, back to the house. From across the field she could see the wisp of blue smoke from the burning old tree. When she arrived it was so hot she could not get near. She settled on a grass blade and called, 'Ann! Ann!' But there was no reply.

All the grasshoppers, bees, ants and butterflies called, 'Ann! Ann, come as fast as you can. Your mother weeps for the frying-pan.'

But the little elf sang a different song. He spied the ladybird Ann sleeping in the cowslip bell and he waved his wand over her. A drop of dew fell from it upon the sleeping ladybird. It washed the cloak, it unglued the seams, and very slowly the cloak changed. Black spots grew on it like circles of embroidery on scarlet silk, and soon there were five clear bright rings of black to make the cloak beautiful. Slowly the wings moved, as the dew moistened them. The ladybird stretched herself, and opened her eyes.

She stood up, spread her wings wide, and then she rose in the air. She could fly! She had wings like her sisters and her wings carried her lightly over the field to her old home. She saw that the house had gone.

Then she spied her mother, weeping softly on a buttercup. 'Mother!' she cried. 'Mother! I can fly.'

'Oh, darling Ann. You can fly. How happy I am,' cried Mrs Ladybird.

'But our house is burnt down,' said Ann sadly.

'We can make another,' said Mrs Ladybird. 'We can have a new house, up in a tree, a May-tree, with little loaves of crimson bread in the autumn, and young fresh leaves in spring. There's such a tree in this field, and it will be covered in May-blossom in a few days.'

'That's the tree where the elf has his house, Mother,' said Ann. 'I once saw him sitting under the boughs and singing. He cured me, Mother, I am sure.'

'Then I will give him the frying-pan,' said Mrs Ladybird.

But when she flew to find the elf he had already found the silver pan. He was stroking the Queen's head and the crown engraved upon it.

'Oh, Mr Elf, I thank you for helping my little Ann. Will you accept that frying-pan from us?'

'Once upon a time my mother had a frying-pan made out of a silver threepenny bit, and we lost it. Now it has come back to us. The date is on it, it is the one we lost,' said the delighted elf.

'And we want to live in your tree, O Elf,' said Ann.

'That will give me great joy,' said the elf. 'I am so lonely. All the elves have gone, and you, Ann Ladybird, will be my friend.'

So Mrs Ladybird made a new house in a branch of the beautiful May-tree, and the butterflies and ants and grass-hoppers all visited her daughter Ann. The elf down below in the ground came up each day and sat in the gnarled roots of the May-tree, singing a little song to Ann, and this is one of his songs:

The Ladybirds

Ladybird Ann has a spotted cloak,
She flies like a bird in the golden smoke,
She darts like a fish in the limpid air,
She is the prettiest fairest fair,
She sleeps in the spotted cowslips' bell,
A ladybird lives in the fairy dell
With an elf, an elf, an elf, who loves her.

The Christmas Surprise

* * *

The clock struck eleven. The kitchen was empty,
except for the cat sitting on the hearth, sleeping
peacefully. The two children and their father were
in bed.

'It's Christmas Eve. Why have you made no
decorations? Why is nothing ready for Christmas
Day?' asked a small indignant voice, as a mouse
squeaked from under a chair.

'Oh, it's you,' muttered the cat, opening one
eye. 'Don't you be too venturesome, even if it is
Christmas Eve. No decorations indeed! Missis is
ill, in hospital. Children can't do things alone.
Mister is very sad.'

'*You* do something,' squeaked the mouse. 'It's
Pax Night tonight, and we'll help you.'

'Pax? Peace? Yes, that's the law tonight. I won't
eat you,' replied the cat. 'Go and get your friends
and relations.'

The mouse ran off, and soon returned with a
host of eager little helpers.

The cat stood up proudly and gave orders.

'Some of you go upstairs and fetch the children's

socks. They will be on the chairs by their beds,'
she commanded.

Away scampered the mice, up the stairs, and
soon came down dragging four socks. The cat hung
the little socks on the clothes-line under the
chimney. 'Now they are ready for the presents,'
she said.

'What presents?' asked the mice.

'Santa Claus will come down the chimney and
bring them presents, to fill their socks,' said the
cat.

'Can we hang our stockings too?' asked the mice.

'If you like,' said the cat.

So the mice took off their furry stockings and hung them by the children's socks.

'What next?' asked the mice.

'Can you cook?' asked the cat.

'Yes, we are very good cooks,' said the mice. 'Toasted cheese, and fried bacon rinds.'

'No, Christmas fare. Can you make mincepies?' The cat opened the larder door and put her paw into a jar of mincemeat. 'Here's flour and lard, to make pastry, and mincemeat to put in it, to make pies. Can you do it, or shall I?'

'Please will you do it, Mistress Cat?' squeaked the mice. So the cat put on a small apron which

hung behind the door and measured out the flour and lard, using her paws.

She made fifty little mincepies each as big as a button, and she turned on the electric cooker and put them in the oven.

'Now for the cake,' said the cat.

'We'll make the cake,' cried the mice quickly. 'We know about cake-making and cake-eating.'

'Currants, raisins, sugar, butter, nuts – nice things to eat,' said one of the mice dreamily, and the rest ran to the larder and dragged out the bags of good things for the cake.

The cat broke the eggs and whisked them to a froth with her paw. The mice measured and mixed the cake with a lot of silver teaspoons, for the long wooden spoon was too heavy for them to lift. Then the cat gave a final swish as she dropped the beaten eggs in the mixture and the cake was put in a tin. The cat carried it to the oven and she lifted out the little mincepies, crisp and delicious.

'While the cake cooks, we can get on with the decorations,' said the cat.

'I can make silver thread,' said a fat old spider who sat in her web. 'Shall I weave some shining threads round the room?'

She spun the long threads, swinging to and fro as she worked, and the beautiful web was drawn across the walls like a silver scarf.

'We will make little baubles to hang on it,' said the mice, and they nibbled some coloured papers

which lay in the corner. They bit the papers into flowery shapes, so that there were pink roses, blue violets and purple and gold lilies, all cut and shaped by their little white teeth. The spider took these blossoms to her web and hung them from it to make a garland.

'We must have a Christmas tree and a kissing bunch,' said the cat. 'I'll go to the wood for holly. All of you get on with the work while I am away. Mind the cake and don't let it burn.'

She leapt out of the window and ran to the woods, and the mice sighed with relief, and went on with their work of flower-making, taking a nibble now and then of the mincepies.

They did not even hear the cat return with her load of holly berries, and her sprays of mistletoe, and the smallest fir-tree, only the size of the cat herself.

So with squeaks of delight they decorated the tree with their own small treasures, and scraps of ribbon, nibbled from a towel. They put the holly sprigs behind the dishes on the dresser, and over the saucepans and the pictures, and the grandfather clock.

'Sniff! Sniff!' went the cat. 'The cake is burning.'

She opened the oven door and took out the crisp sugary-sweet cake with its almonds on the top, and she put it on the prettiest plate she could find. A mouse placed a spray of holly in the middle and they all sat round admiring and smelling.

There was the sound of hoofs and little grunts of the reindeer outside. They all squeaked 'Santa Claus is here.' There was a shuffle in the chimney and they all hid under the chairs, but the cat lay down serenely on the hearth.

Down the chimney came Santa Claus, with a bag on his back. He stepped over the smiling cat and looked around him.

'A Happy Christmas to all within this house,' said he quietly, and to his surprise there were little squeaky voices coming from every corner, little husky voices, excited and queer.

'A Happy Christmas to you, Santa Claus.'

'My goodness! Mice, lots of mice,' said Santa Claus, and he pulled his scarlet robe close to him. He filled the four socks with the nicest toys he could find, and then he sat down in the rocking-chair and sniffed at the cake and tasted a mincepie.

'Now this kitchen is a real home for Santa Claus,' said he. 'I have never seen one quite so pretty as this in all my life. It must have been decorated by the fairies.'

'Miaow,' mewed the cat. 'Not fairies but mice.'

'Not fairies but mice,' echoed Santa Claus.

He reached up to the mouse stockings and in each he dropped a diamond. At least, the tiny things sparkled like diamonds but they may have been magic dewdrops.

'It was lots of mice who did it, and a good kind spider and my humble self,' added the cat.

'Then, Mistress Cat, you shall have a present,' said Santa and he fastened a white velvet collar with a scarlet tassel round the cat's neck and to the spider he gave a tiny crown of rubies.

Then the clock struck twelve, midnight, and Christmas Day came. The mice faded away into their holes, each with his little furry stockings, the spider placed her crown on her head and she returned to her web. The cat lay down by the empty grate, and Santa Claus took up his sack.

He climbed up the chimney and went to the reindeer. 'Christmas Day is here, and even the lowliest creatures have remembered. Come along, my reindeer. Gallop. Gallop to take the good news of Christmas.'

And they flew up in the sky and continued their long journey.